make room for Jake McNair

Writing and Publishing

"Meaningful writing to, for, and from you
to make far-reaching, positive impacts."

www.rejileberje.com

For Joe - there's nobody with whom
I'd rather share the journey of parenthood.
- Reji

For the unwavering support of my wife, Rebecca, and for
my constant muses, Jack and Nick. Woof-woof, Mocha.
- Dah

He's freckled and fair.

She has curly, red hair.

He looks at her
with love and care.

He takes
some boxes up the stairs.
She says, "Darling, I'll be right there."

They have a job, Mr. and Mrs. McNair.

Mr. McNair sits
in the almost empty room.

Except for him there is only
some boxes,
his tools,
and, in the corner, a broom.

Mr. McNair opens the first box and pulls out

pieces of paper;

bits of wood.

Mrs. McNair
comes in,

smiles,

and says,
"Darling, that will
look good."

She carries with her some curtains
in a faded shade of blue.

And the two begin to work
in the almost empty room.

He hammers
while she hums.

She hangs curtains
and pictures
and a mobile.

He hammers top
and bottom,
sides and wheels.

But they still aren't done.

Mr. McNair opens another box and pulls out
pieces of paper;
bits of wood.

He pulls out two blue cushions.
Mrs. McNair says,
"Those look good."

She is holding tiny covers
for a tiny little bed.
And a tiny little pillow
for a tiny little head.

Mr. McNair says,
"Ooh. It's getting crowded in this room."

He hammers
while she hums.

She tucks in pillows
and blankets
and sheets.

He hammers a back
and arm rests
and a seat.

But, they still aren't done.

Mr. McNair opens the last box and pulls out

pieces of paper;

bits of wood.

Mrs. McNair rubs her tummy,
"I think I'll sit," she says,
"That chair looks good."

It is cozy and warm
in the almost full room.

He hammers
while she hums.

She hums rhymes
and songs
and lullabies.

He hammers top
and bottom,
drawers and sides.

And they are almost done.

Mr. McNair picks up his tools,
scraps of paper,
and bits of wood.

Mrs. McNair grabs
empty boxes
and then picks up the broom.

And the two of them clean
the ready little room.

He leaves
and she leaves.

She turns off the light.
She shuts the door.

He says,
"That room needs one thing more."

And when they

open it again . . .

Mr. McNair
turns on the light

and says,

"Look what
we have here."

Mrs. McNair,
with a bundle held tight,
sits in the rocking chair.

He pulls down the crib quilt.
He pulls down the crib sheet.

She says,
"I think this room is complete."

He smiles
while she hums.

She hums to a baby,
a boy
so sweet.

He says,
"You're the one
we've been waiting to meet.

For, now, the room is done."

He's freckled and fair
with curly, red hair.
They look at him with love and care.

"Pleased to meet you," says his mother.
"Happy to greet you," says his father.

Welcome, Welcome, Jake McNair!

www.ingramcontent.com/pod-product-compliance
Lightning Source LLC
Chambersburg PA
CBHW041005170626
46815CB00002B/165

* 9 7 8 0 6 9 2 6 9 7 5 4 2 *